Tales of Tiddly

For Isabelle Holland—DM

For Pam and Peter and Peter—EE

SIMON AND SCHUSTER BOOKS FOR YOUNG READERS

Simon & Schuster Building, Rockefeller Center, 1230 Avenue of the Americas, New York, New York 10020. Copyright © 1990 by Dolores Modrell. Illustrations copyright © 1990 by Ellen Eagle. All rights reserved including the right of reproduction in whole or in part in any form. SIMON AND SCHUSTER BOOKS FOR YOUNG READERS is a trademark of Simon & Schuster Inc.

Designed by Lucille Chomowicz

Manufactured in the United States of America 10 9 8 7 6 5 4 3 2 1

Library of Congress Cataloging-in-Publication Data

Modrell, Dolores. Tales of Tiddly. Summary: Alone in the world, a young cat finds a happy home with Mr. Bones the cat and Uncle Meezo the dog · [1. Cats—Fiction. 2. Dogs—Fiction. 3. Friendship—Fiction.] I. Eagle, Ellen, ill. II. Title. PZ7.M717Tal 1990 [E]—dc20 89-11564 AC ISBN 0-671-69204-6

Tales of Tiddly

by Dolores Modrell
illustrated by Ellen Eagle

SIMON AND SCHUSTER BOOKS FOR YOUNG READERS

Published by Simon & Schuster Inc.
New York • London • Toronto • Sydney • Tokyo • Singapore

Tiddly Finds a Home

Mr. Bones was taking a late afternoon stroll. It had been a lovely spring day. Now, as the shadows lengthened, it was getting cooler.

Mr. Bones walked faster, hurrying along. Suddenly, he stopped. Huddled in a doorway was a small yellow cat.

"Well, I say! What is a little fellow like you doing out here all alone?" said Mr. Bones. "Hadn't you best be getting home? You really shouldn't be here all by yourself, you know. Come, let me walk you to the bus."

"Oh, by the way, my name is Bones, Mr. T. G. Bones. And yours?" Mr. Bones took the yellow cat's paw and pulled him out of the doorway.

"My name is Tiddly, and I would go home if I could, but I don't really have a home to go to." Suddenly, Tiddly was crying.

Mr. Bones put his paws around Tiddly. "There, there,
Tiddly. Stop all this crying. Let's discuss your situation."

"My situation is that I'm tired and cold and hungry,"
said Tiddly. "And I'm scared and I…" Tiddly had to stop
talking because he was crying again.

"Yes. Uh-uh. Well, that is quite a situation." Mr. Bones
said, shaking his head. "Look, Tiddly, I have an idea. I
live with a friend. His name is Uncle Meezo. You can
stay the night, and tomorrow we shall all discuss your
situation. Come along now. And, please, stop that
crying." Mr. Bones took hold of Tiddly's paw and they
started off down the street.

   When they arrived at the house, Mr. Bones
introduced Tiddly to Uncle Meezo. Uncle Meezo had
the kindest face Tiddly had ever seen.
   "Oh, of course, by all means you must stay the night,"
Uncle Meezo said. "Come out to the kitchen right now,
and we'll fix you some supper."

After supper Uncle Meezo showed Tiddly a room
upstairs. "This is where you will sleep, Tiddly," he
explained. "And here is a pair of small pajamas that
I think will fit you."

Uncle Meezo opened a small chest and took out the
pajamas. He bent down and kissed Tiddly on the top
of his head. Then he turned and went down the stairs.

Tiddly was full of good food and so tired he could
hardly stand. He put on the pajamas and jumped into
bed. The next thing he knew, it was morning.

All the next week Tiddly stayed with Uncle Meezo and Mr. Bones. Mr. Bones took him shopping and got him a toothbrush.

Uncle Meezo showed him how to make his bed.

Each day Mr. Bones would say, "Well, now, Uncle Meezo. Isn't it time we discussed Tiddly's situation?"

And each day Uncle Meezo would say, "Let's just wait a day or two, Mr. Bones."

Tiddly liked living with Mr. Bones and Uncle Meezo. He hoped that they would never get around to discussing his situation.

One morning Mr. Bones said, "Tiddly, Uncle Meezo is just outside the front door. I think he has something rather important to show you. Something to do with your situation."

Tiddly's heart started to beat fast. Mr. Bones pointed to the door. Oh, I don't want to have to leave, Tiddly thought.

"Go along, Tiddly; get on with it. Don't keep Uncle Meezo waiting."

Uncle Meezo opened the door. "Good morning, Tiddly. Come out here and see the new nameplate I've just put up."

Tiddly stepped outside. There were three names on the shiny new nameplate:

And that is how Tiddly found a home and two dear friends to live with.

A Day with Himself

Tiddly was brushing his teeth one morning. He looked in the mirror as he brushed. The little yellow cat in the mirror brushed his teeth too. "Who are you, really?" Tiddly asked the mirror. The cat in the mirror mimicked, Who are you, really?

Tiddly turned his back to the mirror. "If I run out of here fast, that cat in the mirror won't know that I've gone." Tiddly dashed out of the bathroom. Outside the door, he peeked around the corner and looked toward the mirror. There in the mirror was a door with a little yellow cat peeking around the corner.

"Come out of there," Tiddly called to the mirror. "What's going on here, Tiddly?" asked Uncle Meezo. "Who are you talking to? I didn't know anyone else was here."

"I'm just talking to myself in the mirror," said Tiddly. "Wouldn't it be nice if the cat in the mirror could get out, and he and I could play together?"

"What? Well, I don't know, really," said Uncle Meezo. He looked in the mirror himself.

"My goodness, who is that handsome dog in the mirror?" he asked. He winked at himself and started to laugh. Tiddly began laughing also, and paw in paw, he and Uncle Meezo headed toward the kitchen and breakfast.

After breakfast Tiddly went outside. He looked
down the empty street. "Where is everybody today?"
he asked, feeling very sorry for himself.
"Now what am I going to do? Who can I play with?"

  "Really, Tiddly," said Mr. Bones. "Do you always have to have someone to play with? When I was a young cat, I very often played by myself all day. It is about time you learned how to do that, too."

  "Mr. Bones is right," said Uncle Meezo. "I think you will find you can have a good time by yourself, Tiddly. Give it a try. Okay?" He patted Tiddly on the head and then gave him a big hug.

  "Well, all right," Tiddly said, "I'm going out. See you later."

Tiddly left the house and wandered down the street. I don't want Mr. Bones and Uncle Meezo to think that I can't have a good time by myself, he thought. But what am I going to do all day?

Just then a bright red car pulled up in front of Tiddly. The driver jumped out and rushed into a house nearby. Tiddly walked up to the car, and there, walking toward him in the shiny side of the car, was—himself!

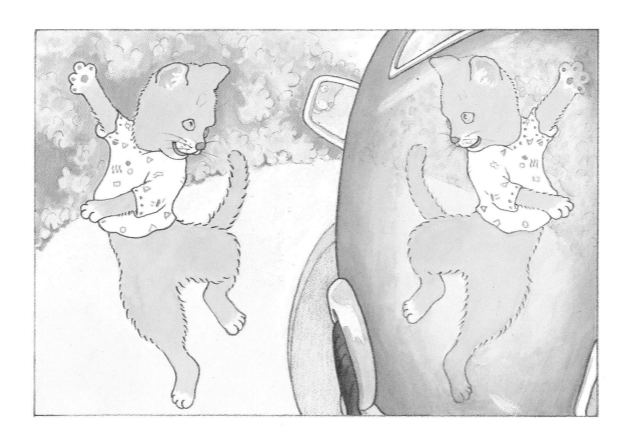

"Oh, for heaven's sake. Me again!" said Tiddly. "This shiny car is just like the mirror this morning." Tiddly bent down to look at himself in the car door.

"I wish you could come out of there and play with me this afternoon," said Tiddly.

The cat in the door bent down, too. Tiddly laughed. The cat in the door laughed back.

Tiddly did a little dance and watched the other cat do the same dance. The driver came back and got into his car. He looked at Tiddly and started to laugh. Tiddly laughed, too. He waved good-bye to himself in the door as the car pulled away from the curb.

Tiddly walked down the street. He came to a store with a big sign that said GALLERY.

Inside were paintings on all the walls. They were in frames with glass on the front. Tiddly was looking at a picture of trees when, suddenly, there he was again!

"Hello, myself," Tiddly said. The little cat in the picture glass said a silent hello back.

Tiddly stood in front of the picture and jumped up and down. "Are you having fun in there?" he asked himself.

The owner of the gallery came running over. "Young cat, young cat. You must be quiet. You are disturbing others." He stood there with his arms folded across his chest.

"Oh, excuse us," said Tiddly. "We're sorry. We didn't mean to be so noisy. We were just leaving anyhow." And he turned and ran out of the gallery.

"We?" the owner said, shaking his head. "We!" He looked very puzzled.

Tiddly walked down the street, stopping every now and then to look at himself in a window. He did several cartwheels with himself in front of one store window, and made faces and stuck out his tongue in front of another.

He came to the park. Tiddly went down to the edge
of a small stream. He leaned over and there, looking up
at him, was himself once again, melting this way and
that in the rippling water.

Tiddly stayed by the stream and watched some birds
bathing. They flew off chattering to one another. The
afternoon passed quickly, and soon it was time to leave.

When Tiddly got home, he was smiling.

"Well, did you have a good time by yourself?"
Mr. Bones asked.

"Yes, I did," Tiddly answered. "I spent the day
with myself and had a very, very good time."

As Tiddly went off to wash up for supper,
Uncle Meezo said, "My, he's a fine little cat, isn't
he, Mr. Bones?"

"Oh, yes, indeed," said Mr. Bones. "A very fine
little cat."

The Christmas Party

Tiddly was hanging the last colored ball on the Christmas tree. The box of decorations was empty, and the tree was full.

"My, that looks nice, Tiddly," said Uncle Meezo. "Do look at the wonderful job Tiddly has done, Mr. Bones."

Mr. Bones walked into the room. "Well done, Tiddly, well done indeed. Say, Uncle Meezo, where did you put those red plates?"

"The plates?" said Uncle Meezo. "Oh dear, I guess
I must have put them back in the cupboard."

"Uncle Meezo, you are getting so forgetful! Did you
remember to get the red napkins out of the cupboard?"
Mr. Bones asked.

"No, was I supposed to?" said Uncle Meezo.

"Well, I had it on my list." Mr. Bones was frowning.

"I forgot to look at the list," Uncle Meezo said.

"Really!" Mr. Bones stamped his foot. The party is
tonight, you know. And we've got a lot to do."

Tiddly went out to the kitchen, where Mr. Bones and Uncle Meezo were getting the plates and napkins out of the cupboard.

"I'm going out to play for a while," Tiddly said. "I've done everything on the list, Mr. Bones."

"Good cat!" Mr. Bones said.

"Bundle up, Tiddly," said Uncle Meezo. "And don't stay out too long. It starts getting dark early, you know."

"All right," said Tiddly. He opened the door to the hall closet and took out his coat and hat and warm mittens. As he reached down to get his boots, he saw a red envelope on the floor.

"What's this?" Tiddly said, picking up the envelope. "Oh, my goodness! It's Old Wiggy's invitation. Uncle Meezo forgot to mail it!"

Uncle Meezo and Old Wiggy had been friends for a very long time. Poor Uncle Meezo, Tiddly thought. He will be so mad at himself. And if Mr. Bones finds out about this....

Suddenly a thought occurred to Tiddly. I know what I'll do, he told himself. I'm a big cat now. I'll deliver the invitation to Old Wiggy myself.

Tiddly got dressed quickly. It was cold outside, and the snow was deep. Tiddly trudged down the street, his tail making a small trail in the snow behind him.

Finally, his tail got so cold that he picked up the end of it and stuffed it into his pocket.

Old Wiggy lived on the other side of the big park. Tiddly had never walked all the way across the park before.

He shivered. Then he took a deep breath of cold air. I'd better get on with it, he said to himself. It's going to start getting dark soon.

He entered the park and found a
path. As he walked along, he listened
to the crunch, crunch of the snow
beneath his feet. On and on he walked
until he reached the far side of the
park and came to Old Wiggy's street.

He looked carefully at the house numbers, and soon
he found Old Wiggy's house. The letter box was up
on the wall. Stretching as high as he could, Tiddly just
managed to reach the box. He dropped the card in.
Then he rushed off the porch and down the street.

Soon he was back in the park, racing along the path
toward home. It was later and darker and colder, but
he was no longer shivering. He was thinking about how
happy Uncle Meezo would be to see Old Wiggy.

At last Tiddly was home again. The three friends got
dressed for the party. Mr. Bones put on his red bow tie.
Uncle Meezo had warm red slippers, and Tiddly had a
new red jacket. When they finished, they all sat down
to have a cup of cocoa.

Soon the doorbell started ringing, and the guests began to arrive. Lots and lots of cats and dogs. Some squirrels and three rabbits. Mr. Bones was very happy. He was busy passing out sandwiches and cookies and pouring cups of hot cocoa.

I wonder where Old Wiggy is? Tiddly thought.

Just then Uncle Meezo put his paw around Tiddly's shoulders. "You don't suppose I forgot to send an invitation to Old Wiggy, do you?"

"Oh, Uncle Meezo," said Tiddly. "He'll be along any minute now, I'm sure." But Tiddly wasn't sure. I hope Old Wiggy looked in his letter box, he thought. Oh dear, what if he didn't get the invitation after all.

The doorbell rang again. "I'll get it," said Uncle Meezo.

"Happy, happy Christmas, Meezo!" called Old Wiggy as he rushed into the room.

"What a welcome sight you are, Wiggy!" Uncle Meezo called back.

The two old friends laughed and hugged and hugged some more. Then they joined Mr. Bones and the others.

Tiddly saw that the front door was standing open. Uncle Meezo had forgotten to shut it.

He stepped onto the porch. Snowflakes were dancing as the light from the porch spread out against the night.

In the porch light Tiddly could just read the nameplate on the door.

He stood for a moment, smiling, and then he entered the warm house, gently closing the door behind him.